JUSTICE™ LEAGUE

GORILLA GRODD
AND THE
PRIMATE PROTOCOL

raintree

Published by Raintree, an imprint of Capstone Global Library Limited, a company incorporated in England and Wales having its registered office at 264 Banbury Road, Oxford, OX2 7DY – Registered company number: 6695582

www.raintree.co.uk
myorders@raintree.co.uk

STAR40489

ISBN 978 1 4747 5479 8
22 21 20 19 18
10 9 8 7 6 5 4 3 2 1

A full catalogue record for this book is available from the British Library.

Editor: Christopher Harbo
Designer: Bob Lentz

Printed and bound in India.

CONTENTS

When the champions of Earth came together to battle a threat too big for a single hero, they realized the value of strength in numbers. Together they formed an unstoppable team, dedicated to defending the planet from the forces of evil. They are the . . .

JUSTICE LEAGUE™

{ MEMBERS }

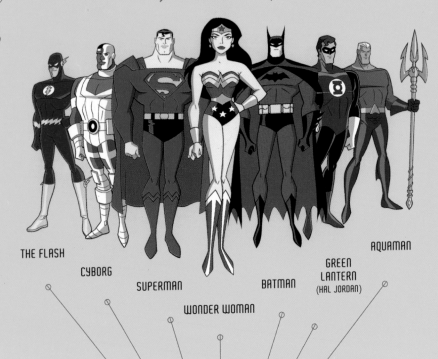

THE FLASH

CYBORG

SUPERMAN

WONDER WOMAN

BATMAN

GREEN LANTERN (HAL JORDAN)

AQUAMAN

MARTIAN
MANHUNTER

HAWKGIRL

HAWKMAN

GREEN ARROW

BLACK CANARY

GREEN LANTERN
(JOHN STEWART)

THE ATOM

SUPERGIRL

RED TORNADO

POWER GIRL

SHAZAM

PLASTIC MAN

BOOSTER GOLD

BLUE BEETLE

ZATANNA

VIXEN

METAMORPHO

ETRIGAN
THE DEMON

FIRESTORM

HUNTRESS

CHAPTER 1

NEVER-ENDING BATTLE

BEEP! BEEP! BEEP!

Batman scrambled to answer the blaring Trouble Alert as it filled the corridors of the Justice League's orbital Watchtower. He'd been on monitoring duty for hours, directing Justice League members across the globe. Some were handling natural disasters while others were stopping crime sprees. With so many emergencies to deal with, the team was spread thin. Though Batman kept his cool, the pressures of command weighed heavily on his shoulders.

"Attention: Justice League. All active members who are *not* working in the field, return to the Watchtower immediately," Batman commanded into the Watchtower's communications system. "We need all the help we can get."

"We're about to head out to the Galactic Peace Conference," Superman said, entering the control centre with Cyborg. "If you need us to stick around, we're happy to do it."

"That won't be necessary," Batman said. "You've got your mission. I've got everything under control here."

"Are you *sure* about that?" Cyborg asked. "Say the word. We've got your back."

"Galactic peace is more important," Batman said. "A handful of members should be arriving soon."

BEEP! BEEP! BEEP!

The Flash raced in as the Trouble Alert went off again. "You really should answer that, Batman. It could be urgent," he said with a smile.

"Let him work, Flash. We're expected elsewhere," said Superman. "See you soon, Batman. Good luck with everything!"

BOOM!

In an instant, Superman, Cyborg and The Flash teleported to the far side of the galaxy, leaving Batman to attend to the distress call.

BEEP! BEEP! BEEP!

Batman pushed a button and Wonder Woman appeared on screen. She was in the middle of a fierce battle against a group of masked men. "Go ahead, Wonder Woman," Batman said. "What's your emergency?"

"I'm at the Gateway City armoury," said Wonder Woman. Lasers fired at her from all directions. She easily deflected the blasts with her silver bracelets. "Soldiers are stealing advanced weaponry. I need backup *now*."

"Backup isn't an option, but I may be able to help," Batman said. He used the Watchtower's advanced computer to scan Wonder Woman's enemies. "Those soldiers you're up against aren't human – they're androids. I suspect they're programmed to keep going until they complete their mission. You've definitely got your hands full."

"If they're androids, I don't have to pull any punches," said Wonder Woman. "I can take them all out."

"Correct," Batman replied. "Though I'd appreciate it if you brought me back a piece of one so I can study its mechanics."

Wonder Woman nodded. "I'll see what I can do." Batman watched as the Amazing Amazon jumped into action, battling through the robot army, throwing them around like rag dolls.

BEEP! BEEP! BEEP!

Another alert meant another crisis was brewing. Before Batman could handle it, Hawkman and Green Lantern returned from a mission in deep space.

"Fighting those lizard men from the planet Gordane was exhausting," Green Lantern said, collapsing into a seat at the team's meeting table.

"Agreed, John. Gordanians are disgusting creatures. The universe is better off when they're broken and defeated," Hawkman said, removing his helmet.

SNIFF! SNIFF!

Green Lantern wrinkled his nose. "Oh great. Some of their stink must have rubbed off on me. I need a shower."

"Don't go *anywhere*," said Batman. "The team needs you both to remain at the ready until more members become available."

A short time later, Wonder Woman arrived. She placed a robotic-looking arm on the meeting table. "They put up a good fight," she said. "Is *this* suitable for studying?"

Batman looked pleased. "Nice work," he said.

Green Arrow, Vixen and Firestorm rushed into the control room. They had received Batman's message and answered the call of duty as soon as possible.

"Hey, everyone! Looks like a party," said Firestorm. "I hope there's cake. Though I'm more of an ice cream guy."

Hawkman wasn't in a joking mood. "This is *serious*, Firestorm," he growled.

"Give the kid a break. He's just trying to lighten things up," said Green Arrow. "What's up, Batman? You rang, we answered."

BEEP! BEEP! BEEP!

The Trouble Alert sounded once more. It was a direct message from Solovar, the leader of Gorilla City.

"Greetings, Batman. I wish I brought good news," Solovar began. "Grodd has escaped prison and is loose in Gorilla City again."

"How could that happen?" asked Green Arrow. "We put your people in charge of keeping Grodd locked up."

"Quiet!" snapped Hawkman. "Let Solovar speak."

"He slipped through our fingers despite our best efforts. Grodd's mental powers are weakened but that won't last long. During the breakout he stole the helmet he uses to strengthen his ability to control people. With it he could become unstoppable," said Solovar. "I speak on behalf of all Gorilla City. We need your help now more than ever."

Batman thought for a moment. The timing was terrible, but he wasn't about to let Solovar down.

"You've been an ally to the League, Solovar," Batman said. "We'll send a group to Gorilla City to help track down Grodd and bring him to the US. That way we can lock him up safely and keep him out of your hair once and for all."

"That's a lot of hair," Green Arrow said. "You know, since he's a *gorilla*."

"You just don't know when to keep your mouth shut, do you, Arrow?" barked Hawkman.

"Enough," Batman said. "We don't have time for bickering. Stay focused."

"Be safe, Solovar. We'll see you soon, old friend," Wonder Woman said, ending the transmission.

"We could be walking into a trap. Grodd is crafty like that," said Vixen. "Are we sure that Solovar isn't under his spell?"

"Good point. That's why I watched Solovar's actions and speech, looking for anything out of the ordinary. Based on what I saw, he doesn't appear to be controlled in any way," said Batman.

Firestorm felt nervous. As one of the Justice League's newest heroes, he hadn't worked with many of the team's core members. *What if they ask me to go on this mission?* he thought. *I'm not prepared!*

Luckily, he had an extra bit of help: Professor Martin Stein. Firestorm was created when a laboratory explosion merged the Professor with student Ronnie Raymond. While Ronnie controlled Firestorm's physical body, the Professor guided his mind telepathically. No one else could see or hear him, but the Professor was always there.

"I don't know about this," Firestorm muttered to himself.

"Relax, Ronald," said Professor Stein. "You can do this."

Batman took charge of the situation.

"Listen up, everyone. Wonder Woman will lead the mission to Gorilla City," Batman explained. "Vixen will serve as second-in-command. She can channel the powers of the animal kingdom. That makes her your best asset for tracking Grodd."

"Wait a minute," said Green Lantern. "Since I'm a full-time Leaguer, shouldn't *I* be second-in-command?"

Vixen smiled. "It's been a long time since we've worked together, Green Lantern. Don't worry, I can handle the job," she said. "I've been a hero just as long as you have."

"Green Lantern will help with team coordination," Batman continued. "Firestorm will also join you. He can transmute elements, which may come in handy. Despite his inexperience, there's a genius giving him advice inside his head."

"Professor Stein says hi, Batman!" said Firestorm.

"Ah yes. The man with two brains," said Hawkman.

"Nope, only one brain! Professor Stein and I share it," Firestorm explained.

"What does *transmute* mean anyway?" asked Green Arrow.

"It means I can rearrange the molecules in non-living objects," Firestorm explained. "Basically, I can change stuff into different stuff. Professor Stein helps me do that because he's a science guy."

Wonder Woman wasn't so sure about including Firestorm. "With or without his mental powers, Grodd can be very controlling," she said. "Is it wise to have such a young member on a dangerous mission?"

"Firestorm may be learning to use his powers, but Professor Stein has always steered him in the right direction," Batman said. "I'm certain he'll do just fine."

"Let's get going," Wonder Woman said. "Since it's just us four, we can take my jet."

"One moment, Wonder Woman," Batman said. He hadn't quite finished selecting the squad. "Hawkman and Green Arrow will also join you. Green Arrow is an expert marksman and Hawkman is a powerful fighter."

"Why do I have to work with this winged barbarian?" Green Arrow exclaimed.

"Must you always be so unbearably annoying, Green Arrow?" Hawkman growled.

"Respect one another. We're all super heroes here. Act like it," said Vixen.

Wonder Woman was impressed by Vixen's take-charge attitude. "Exactly," she said. "It's crucial that we have each other's backs."

Batman had one last piece of advice before they left. "Don't underestimate Grodd. He's sneaky and an expert planner. Stay alert," he said. "Bring back that helmet in one piece so I can take it apart for good."

"Oh, I'll stay alert, all right," said Green Arrow, leaning into Hawkman's face. "I've got to keep my eye on this guy."

"Conflict can be good," said Batman. "But finding common ground will make you a stronger team."

"We'll make do with what we have," said Wonder Woman. "Let's go."

The team piled into the Javelin, the Justice League's spacecraft, and left for Gorilla City.

CHAPTER 2
AMBUSH

"We're approaching Gorilla City," Green Lantern said. He flipped a switch in the Javelin's cockpit, activating a hologram of Grodd. The team gathered around as Wonder Woman briefed them on their enemy.

"Grodd isn't known as a fighter, but he's still a force to be reckoned with. He likes commanding his minions to do his dirty work through mind control. He's also been known to control people by using their insecurities against them," said Wonder Woman.

"What if we don't have any insecurities?" asked Green Arrow.

"Don't interrupt, Arrow," said Hawkman.

"Grodd blames the Justice League for being sent to prison," Wonder Woman said, continuing her briefing. "He's vowed revenge on us and won't give up easily. All of you must be on guard at all times."

"Um, excuse me, Wonder Woman. What do we do if Grodd tries to take control of *our* minds?" asked Firestorm.

The team fell silent. They all knew this mission was filled with danger. The thought of having their minds taken over by Grodd sent chills down their spines.

"Fight to remember who you are and what you stand for," said Wonder Woman. "It won't be easy but hold on."

"No gorilla is taking over *my* noggin, that's for sure," said Green Arrow.

"Don't be so sure," Vixen disagreed. "Grodd doesn't need superpowers to control minds," Vixen said. "He's a master at getting people to do what he wants even without his mental powers."

"We're here," said Green Lantern. He landed the Javelin in the middle of Gorilla City's capital square where Solovar was waiting. The stately gorilla leader was flanked by bodyguards wearing bulky battle armour and carrying ceremonial spears.

Firestorm was in complete awe of his new surroundings. "This is so cool!" he exclaimed. "It's like the future and the past smashed together. They've got tree houses that look like spaceships!"

"Stay sharp, Ronald. We're in unfamiliar territory," said Professor Stein. "Looks may be deceiving."

Solovar greeted the team with open arms. "Welcome, Justice League," he said. "It's good to see you, even in times of trouble."

"We're always here to help, Solovar," said Wonder Woman. "Tell us what happened."

"We'd been keeping Grodd in a maximum-security prison where we used a power dampening device to keep his mental abilities in a weakened state. But that didn't stop him from tricking one of the guards into letting him out," Solovar explained.

"See, Green Arrow? I told you he doesn't need powers to control people," said Vixen.

"Well, he won't get into my head with his sweet talk," Green Arrow said with a wink.

"Grodd uses a special helmet to boost his powers. We kept it locked up, but he stole it back after his escape," explained Solovar.

"We won't let you down, Solovar," said Hawkman. "I'll take to the skies and see if I can spot him from above."

"What we *need* to do is stay on the ground and look for this guy on foot," Green Arrow said. "A view from above won't do us any good if he's hiding."

Vixen's body glowed with pulsing, purple energy. She used her animal power to channel the tracking skills of a wolf.

"It's too late," Vixen exclaimed. "Grodd is already here! I can smell him."

Everyone stood motionless. But after a few moments of silence, Grodd had yet to appear.

"So where is he?" asked Green Arrow.

Then Firestorm noticed Solovar's guards twitching their bodies strangely. "Are they okay?" he asked.

"Ooook," muttered a bodyguard.

"Ooook! Ooook!" exclaimed another.

"Grodd is controlling their minds," Wonder Woman said. "Everyone brace yourselves for an attack!"

CLAP! CLAP! CLAP!

The sound of applause echoed from the trees above. Grodd was amused. He swung down on a jungle vine, landing in the middle of the group. "Hello, Justice League. You're correct, Wonder Woman. I now control my gorilla brothers," he said. "But are you sure I haven't come in peace? Looks can be deceiving, after all."

"End this nonsense, Grodd!" Solovar said. "You're surrounded and out of options."

"I don't think I am, Solovar," Grodd sneered.

Solovar jerked his body back and forth, grabbing his head in agony. "Gahhhh!!!" he cried. "He's . . . taking . . . over . . . my body!" Suddenly the twitching stopped as Solovar's body went limp. He was completely under Grodd's control. "Ooook?" he muttered.

"We're in deep trouble," said Green Arrow.

"Hurt them, my brothers!" Grodd shouted, disappearing into the trees. Solovar's mind-controlled bodyguards raised their spears and charged towards the Justice League in full force.

"Spread out!" exclaimed Wonder Woman.

"RARGH!" growled one gorilla as he rushed Green Lantern. The emerald warrior used his ring to create a shield that blocked the beast from smashing him to pieces.

"Time to get creative," Green Lantern said.

Long, curling tendrils sprung from Green Lantern's shield and wrapped themselves around the angry gorilla. Soon the beast was covered in a glowing green cocoon.

"That should hold you," said Green Lantern.

To avoid capture, Green Arrow shot a cable into a nearby tree and swung up onto one of its branches. "How do you like me *now?*" he taunted the gorillas below. They weren't amused and soon began climbing the tree to retrieve him.

Green Arrow reached into his quiver and began shooting his trick arrows one after the other. A Boxing Glove Arrow hit one gorilla in the nose, sending him falling to the ground. Another gorilla caught an Electric Shock Arrow and was zapped with 1,000 volts of electricity.

While Green Arrow wasn't looking, a different gorilla snuck up behind him. It smashed the hero's quiver to pieces, leaving him arrowless.

"Be a nice boy, huh?" Green Arrow whispered as the creature lunged at him.

Out of nowhere, Hawkman swooped in. He used his silver mace to swat the angry gorilla out of the tree with a loud *THWACK!*

"You can thank me for saving you later!" Hawkman shouted, soaring away into the sky. "We've got work to do first."

On the ground, Wonder Woman was battling two gorillas at once. While she blocked an attack from one gorilla, she used her lasso to entangle the other. *These beasts aren't in control of themselves,* she thought. *I don't want to hurt them, but they leave me no choice.*

Wonder Woman grabbed the gorillas and swung them into one another, knocking them out.

Solovar slowly approached Wonder Woman as she took a moment to catch her breath. His eyes were deep red. "Wonder Woman," he growled, baring his sharp teeth. "Must destroy Wonder Woman."

"Your mind is not your own, Solovar," said Wonder Woman. "Fight Grodd's control. I know you can do it!"

Wonder Woman whirled her lasso towards the brutish gorilla, hoping to ensnare him. Instead he grabbed it and yanked her into the surrounding jungle.

Firestorm stood guard over the Javelin in case Grodd tried to use it to make an escape. After watching Solovar take down Wonder Woman, he knew he had to join the battle.

"Hey, you big, dumb ape!" Firestorm shouted. "Pick on someone your own size."

"RARGH!" Solovar screamed, charging Firestorm with renewed anger.

"What should I do, Professor? I've never fought a rampaging gorilla!" Firestorm exclaimed. "Maybe I should change the ground to something else."

"Do it quickly, Ronald!" said the Professor.

Firestorm's hands glowed yellow as a burst of atomic energy changed the solid ground in front of him into a bubbling pool of quicksand. As soon as Solovar stepped into it, he sank to his waist and got stuck.

Grodd had been watching Firestorm closely from his jungle perch. *That young man is very powerful,* he thought. *I may be able to use him to my advantage.*

Luckily, Green Lantern stepped in to help. He used his ring to create a brand-new bow and Boxing Glove Arrow. "I hope this'll do," he said.

"It's perfect," said Green Arrow. He focused his aim and shot the arrow, knocking Grodd out cold. The giant gorilla fell to the ground with a *THUD*.

"Hawkman and Green Arrow, help get Grodd into the Javelin's prison cell. Firestorm, make sure his helmet is completely secure. Vixen and Green Lantern, prepare the Javelin for take-off," said Wonder Woman. "Nice work, everyone. Let's head home."

CHAPTER 3

MASTER PLAN REVEALED

Wonder Woman stared at Grodd as he sat in his prison cell. *I hope this is strong enough to hold him,* she thought.

Grodd was groggy, having just woken up. "Where's my helmet?" he asked.

"This ol' thing?" Firestorm said, holding the helmet in the air. "You won't be getting your paws on this again, that's for sure. Wait. Do gorillas have paws?"

"No, Ronald," said Professor Stein. "They have five fingers, including an opposable thumb, just like humans do."

Wonder Woman watched Grodd stare at the helmet in Firestorm's hands. It made her uneasy. "Firestorm, take that device somewhere else, please," she said.

"Be careful with it," said Grodd.

"You don't need to worry about that," Wonder Woman said. "You'll never use this helmet again once Batman takes it apart."

"I'm not worried, Wonder Woman," Grodd said as a smile formed on his face. "But you should be. During your battle with my gorilla brothers, I saw a ferocious side of you I hadn't seen before. Give in to it. Let go of that stuffy Amazonian training. Be free."

"You can't manipulate me," she said. "I don't give in to my animal instincts."

"Ha, ha, ha!" cackled Grodd. "We'll see about that."

Wonder Woman had had enough of Grodd's games. "Firestorm, keep an eye on him for the rest of our journey," she said. "Be *very* careful. Watch him like a hawk."

"Hey, Wonder Woman? I can't channel animal powers. That's Vixen's thing. I think you might be getting us mixed up," Firestorm said as a confused look crossed his face.

"I didn't mean for you to *actually* watch him like a hawk. It's just an expression," Wonder Woman said. "I need you to make sure he doesn't get up to anything."

"Oh! OH! Ha, ha, ha! I get it. That's good. You're funny," Firestorm said. He was nervous and sweating like crazy.

"Take a deep breath," Wonder Woman said. "Clear your mind. Focus on the task you've been given, and you'll be fine."

"Got it, Wonder Woman," Firestorm said, shaking his hands and cracking his neck like a boxer. "Thanks for the pep talk."

In the middle of the Javelin, Green Arrow kicked his feet up. He was ready to relax after an exhausting battle. "That was crazy. Those gorillas were a real bunch of, well, gorillas," he said. "I wonder how many bananas they go through in a day."

Hawkman silently polished his mace, ignoring Green Arrow's babbling.

"What's your problem, huh?" Green Arrow asked.

Hawkman furrowed his brow. "You talk too much," he said.

"I'm just trying to have a little fun, man," Green Arrow scoffed. "This hero thing can get pretty intense. Loosen up, why don't you?"

Wonder Woman overheard their conversation and stepped in to offer a bit of advice. "I saw you both work together in battle. You had each other's backs, as I knew you would. Teammates don't always need to get along, but when a problem arises, solve it. Do not let it fester," she explained.

Green Arrow seemed anxious. He wanted to say something but was holding back. "So, um, Hawkman, thanks for smurvymerbuherr," he muttered.

"What was that? I can't hear you," said Hawkman.

"I said *thanks for saving my behind!*" exclaimed Green Arrow. "There. Are you happy now?"

Hawkman smiled. "You're welcome," he replied.

He put on quite a show of power back in Gorilla City, but now he's anxious and avoiding eye contact, Grodd thought. *The boy is afraid of me. I can use that to my advantage.*

Firestorm did his best to play it cool. "Hey, um, Professor, when we get back to the Watchtower, I might need your help with my homework," he said. "There are a couple of questions I had about calculus. Namely, what is it?"

"I'm happy to help, Ronald," said Professor Stein.

Grodd was desperate for more information about Firestorm's unique relationship with Professor Stein.

"Tell me about this Professor you keep speaking to," said Grodd. "He speaks to you inside your mind, yes?"

Firestorm shuddered. "I shouldn't be talking to you," he said.

"Why is that? I'm not powerful enough to take over your mind. Not without my helmet," said Grodd. "Don't be so afraid. I can't control you."

"That's right, you can't control me!" exclaimed Firestorm.

"Take it easy, Ronald," said Professor Stein. "Don't let him rile you."

"You're the most powerful person here, Firestorm. You can make almost anything you want, yet you fear using your abilities. Why is that?" asked Grodd. "I think it's because these other heroes are holding you back. Embrace your gifts. Show them who you really are."

BEEP! BEEP! BEEP!

Suddenly, Grodd's helmet began beeping. Hawkman, Wonder Woman and Green Arrow huddled around it to try to work out what was wrong.

"Is it a short circuit? Someone help me out here. I'm not really a science guy," said Green Arrow.

Grodd nodded at Firestorm. "You know about science, don't you?" he said. "Or at least your friend, the Professor, does."

Grodd's right, thought Firestorm, *even though I hate to admit that.* He joined his teammates to review the strange device. "Hmm," he said. "Looks like it's been tinkered with in some way."

"Uh-oh. My ring is picking up something weird," Green Lantern said. "I think you guys might want to step away from that helmet."

"Fools. You played right into my trap," growled Grodd.

BEEP! BEEP! BEEP!

The helmet's signal grew louder until finally it released a pulse of strange energy. It bathed the inside of the Javelin in a bright light. **FWASH!**

Thanks to Green Lantern's quick thinking, he avoided the energy pulse. He used his ring to create an emerald bubble that protected him and Vixen from the blast.

The other Leaguers weren't so lucky. They jerked back and forth as their bodies grew to an enormous size. In an instant, thick, black hair sprouted from their arms and legs. They bared their sharp teeth in anger. Wonder Woman, Green Arrow, Hawkman and Firestorm had transformed into mindless gorillas! And they were about to attack.

"This is *not* good," Green Lantern said. He quickly scrambled to contact the Watchtower. "This is Green Lantern. We've got a big problem, Batman. That helmet you were curious about just changed everyone except Vixen and me into gorillas."

"RARGH!" screamed Hawkman. He used his mace to smash the communication system, ending Green Lantern's distress call.

"This must have been Grodd's plan all along," said Vixen.

Grodd cackled from inside his cell. "Ha, ha, ha! Of course it was! Stupid human. I adjusted my helmet and used it as a time bomb," he sneered. "That's what a *true* genius does. Now free me, Firestorm!"

"Ooook!" barked Firestorm. He focused his powers and turned Grodd's metal prison cell into a pile of straw.

Wonder Woman had her eye on Vixen and rushed towards her.

"Diana, stop!" Vixen exclaimed. She leaped into the air to avoid Wonder Woman's attack. "We've fought together many times. You're like family to me," she said. "Just remember that because you're not going to like what I do next."

Vixen cleared her mind and channelled the power of a rhino. She charged Wonder Woman, knocking her off her feet and into the rear of the ship.

Green Arrow angrily ripped apart the interior of the Javelin. In his mindless rage he accidentally tore a hole in the ship's hull, causing it to lose pressure.

"You idiot!" Grodd exclaimed. He grabbed his helmet and placed it on his head. "Firestorm, use your powers to fix that hole."

Coating his body in emerald light, Green Lantern phased through the roof of the Javelin. The ship was heading straight towards the heart of New York City. He stood atop the Javelin like a surfer, using his ring to create a pair of thick glowing cables. He swung them around the nose of the spacecraft to help guide it, but the ship wasn't slowing down.

If I'm going to tame this thing, I'll need to pull out all the stops, he thought.

Green Lantern created two giant jet engines on either side of the ship. He fired up the thrusters in reverse, which helped break the ship's fall.

"C'mon!" he strained, guiding the Javelin safely down into the middle of Central Park.

He'd saved the team, but the danger was far from over.

CHAPTER 4

RAMPAGE

RARGH!

Wonder Woman screeched, then she burst from the side of the Javelin with Green Arrow, Hawkman and Firestorm following behind. They violently stomped away, scrambling onto the streets of New York City while Grodd slipped out in secret.

Vixen rubbed her head as she slowly made her way out of the Javelin.

"Are you all right?" asked Green Lantern.

"I'll be fine," she said.

Green Lantern and Vixen looked out among the trees of Central Park, but their gorilla friends had already disappeared. Grodd was nowhere to be seen. As civilians began to gather, the two heroes realized the game had changed.

"Now that we're in a populated area, there's no telling what kind of trouble those gorillas will get into. We need to stop them before they hurt someone," said Green Lantern. "I'll use my ring to contact Batman. We're going to need reinforcements."

"You don't get it, John," Vixen said as she looked Green Lantern square in the eye. "It's just you and me out here. Everyone else is busy saving the world. It's up to us."

"You're right," Green Lantern agreed. "So, what's our strategy?"

Vixen closed her eyes. She used her power to channel the tracking abilities of a wolf. "I know which direction Grodd went," she said.

"Ahhhhhhh! A gorilla with wings!" a woman screamed.

"Help! It wants to eat me!" yelled another.

"It sounds like our friends are up to no good. Grodd will have to wait," said Green Lantern. "People need our protection first."

"I'll handle Hawkman and Green Arrow. I've got their scent," Vixen said. "You handle Wonder Woman and Firestorm."

"How am I supposed to find them?" asked Green Lantern.

Vixen pointed to a nearby building. Wonder Woman was climbing it, smashing windows as she went. "Good luck," Vixen said. "You're going to need it."

"What about Firestorm?" asked Green Lantern.

"He'll turn up soon enough," Vixen said. "Remember, Professor Stein is rattling around in his head. Hopefully the Professor can help steer him away from trouble."

Green Lantern took off into the sky to stop Wonder Woman while Vixen raced after Green Arrow and Hawkman.

* * *

"Ooook! Ooook?" Firestorm muttered. He'd been hiding in a huge bin behind a restaurant, frightened and confused. While his teammates had fallen to Grodd's gorilla bomb, Firestorm still had his mental bond with Professor Stein. His body had turned into a gorilla, but the Professor's brilliant mind wasn't going down without a fight.

"Calm yourself, Ronald. Take a deep breath," comforted Professor Stein. "Listen to my voice and everything will be okay."

Firestorm's eyebrow rose with curiosity. "Man . . . inside . . . head?" he asked.

"Indeed, I am!" Professor Stein exclaimed. *This is wonderful,* he thought. *Ronald can still hear me, which means there's a chance I can save him.*

Firestorm peeked out of the bin just as the restaurant's cook was about to throw a bag of rubbish into it.

"GAH! A gorilla with a flaming head!" the cook screamed. He dropped the bag, spilling its contents on the ground before running back inside.

Firestorm climbed out and rummaged through the pile of rubbish. He was looking for something to eat.

"Oh no. No, no, no. Don't do that, Ronald. Bad gorilla!" said Professor Stein.

"Me bad?" asked Firestorm. "Like Grodd?"

Oh dear. What have I got myself into? thought Professor Stein. *It won't be easy to tame this wild beast. I hope the rest of the team is faring better than I am.*

* * *

On the Upper East Side of Manhattan, Green Lantern was busy using his ring to pry Wonder Woman from the side of a building. He'd made a giant emerald crowbar, but it wasn't much use. Her massive gorilla body, combined with her Amazonian strength, made her a force to be reckoned with. She grabbed the crowbar and broke it in half.

"Puny!" she barked.

"How did you do that?" Green Lantern asked.

Grodd watched the battle from nearby. He'd positioned himself on the edge of Central Park and was hiding in a tree. His helmet allowed him to control the gorilla Leaguers remotely, but in this case he preferred to watch his handiwork in person.

"RARGH!" cried Wonder Woman. She pounded the brick wall, sending debris hurtling towards the ground. Green Lantern created a giant spider's web near the base of the building that safely collected the falling rubble so it wouldn't hurt anyone.

Wonder Woman's eyes darted from place to place. She searched for her next target. She jumped from the building and began stomping down the street. Frightened citizens ran in every direction to escape her fury.

I need to distract her so she focuses her attention away from the people, Green Lantern thought. *I suppose that means I'll have to direct her attention towards me.*

Green Lantern used his ring to create a mask that covered Wonder Woman's eyes. She didn't like that one bit.

"Ooook!" Wonder Woman yelped, swiping at the mask and struggling to take it off.

Annoyed by her lack of sight, Wonder Woman stretched out her arms to feel her surroundings. Her hands soon found an empty dumper truck. She grabbed it by the bumper and hoisted it high into the air.

"Don't you do what I think you're about to do!" exclaimed Green Lantern. He removed the mask from Wonder Woman's eyes, hoping it would stop her.

"Is that better?" he asked. "Come on, Diana. Calm down for a minute. Let's work this out. We're friends. You're not going to let Grodd win, are you?"

Wonder Woman hesitated for a moment. She placed the truck back on the ground safely. "Green . . . Lantern?" she mumbled.

"Yes!" exclaimed Green Lantern. "I knew you were in there somewhere."

Grodd fumed. He didn't expect Wonder Woman's mind to be so strong. He quickly tightened his mental grip, jolting her from the peaceful moment. She grabbed the dumper truck once more and threw it towards a group of onlookers.

"I spoke too soon," said Green Lantern. He quickly created a giant emerald catapult. It caught the truck and threw it back at Wonder Woman, knocking her off her feet.

While she was dazed, Green Lantern used his ring to shackle her limbs tightly. "You might break out of these, but I'll be right here to put you back," he said.

With the struggle at an end, Grodd took off across the park, heading east.

*   *   *

Firestorm lumbered down 5th Avenue, watching frightened citizens run for cover. He felt confused. He knew they feared him, but he wasn't sure why. Inside his head Professor Stein struggled to reach his human side.

"Ronald, listen to me. Your teammates need you to fight Grodd's control! You have the power to stop him, but you'll have to concentrate," said Professor Stein.

"Man . . . in head . . . stop . . . talking!" Firestorm exclaimed. "RARGH!"

Firestorm smashed a shop window. Then he kicked a fire hydrant, causing a burst of water to spurt into the air.

"Focus," Professor Stein said. "You're a hero, Ronald Raymond. It's time for you to rise to the occasion."

In an instant Firestorm was calmer. He shook out of his anger, newly aware of his surroundings. "Professor? Where am I?" he asked, looking around with confusion.

"You did it, Ronald!" exclaimed Professor Stein. "You successfully broke through Grodd's control! I knew you could do it."

Firestorm noticed his gorilla body and was shocked. "What the what?! How did I become a big, hairy beast?!" he asked. "The last thing I remember was talking to Grodd on the Javelin. There was a burst of light and then *poof!*"

"Grodd's helmet was booby trapped. Hawkman, Green Arrow and Wonder Woman were also turned into gorillas. We need to find Grodd and use his helmet to change them back," explained the Professor. "Gorillas have a keen sense of smell. Perhaps you can use yours to track down Grodd?"

SNIFF! SNIFF! SNIFF!

"There!" Firestorm shouted. He pointed towards the New York Public Library where people were fleeing in droves.

"A brilliant deduction, Ronald! Grodd is a student of history and war. He's probably studying library books looking for ways to defeat humanity," said Professor Stein.

"I thought he was probably in there because people were running for their lives," said Firestorm. "But the thing about studying war sounds good too."

Nearby, Vixen chased Green Arrow on foot, zigzagging through the streets of the city. She'd been channelling the powers of a gorilla, but it was time to shake things up.

I'll need to go faster if I want to catch him, Vixen thought. She felt a jolt of energy rush through her body as she channelled the speed of a cheetah. With a burst of power, she launched onto Green Arrow's back.

"RARGH!" he cried. "Get . . . off!" Green Arrow tried to buck Vixen away, but her grip was too strong.

Hawkman had been watching from the sky above. He swiftly swooped down and snatched Vixen off Green Arrow's back. She struggled to free herself.

He's going to fly as high as he can and then drop me, Vixen thought. *It's a good thing I've got the entire animal kingdom at my fingertips.*

Hawkman flew high above the city. *It's now or never,* Vixen thought. She channelled the power of a wolverine and scraped Hawkman's hands with her sharp claws. As he lost his grip, he threw her towards the ground in anger.

Vixen closed her eyes and channelled the power of a flying squirrel. She glided through the air with ease, landing safely in the middle of Times Square. Panicked tourists ran in all directions. Green Arrow was already there waiting for her, and he wasn't about to back down.

Hawkman spotted the battle from above and dove down from the sky. He pushed Green Arrow aside, knocking him into a building.

"She mine!" barked Hawkman.

"No! She mine!" yelled Green Arrow. He hopped on Hawkman's back and began pounding him with his fists.

Hawkman bolted into the air, hoping to shake off the attack. Green Arrow awkwardly climbed onto Hawkman's chest and gave him a series of powerful headbutts. The blows eventually knocked Hawkman out, sending him plummeting to the ground where he fell on top of Green Arrow.

Unbelievable, thought Vixen. *Even as gorillas they have trouble getting along.*

* * *

At the New York Public Library, Firestorm found Grodd reading peacefully in the corner. "Hello, young man. I've been expecting you," he said. "It seems my presence upset the other readers. Oh well. I've been waiting to have some alone time with you."

"Ooook?" muttered Firestorm.

"I'm studying your American history. What a fascinating thing," Grodd said. "I believe I'm going to enjoy taking over this country and turning it into a new Gorilla Colony."

Firestorm grew anxious. "Ooook! Ooook, oook!" he exclaimed.

Grodd smiled. "I can sense you in there, Professor Stein, trying to break through my control," said Grodd. "Give up. Firestorm is mine now. Isn't that right?"

"Ooo, ooo, ooo! Ahhh, ahhh, ahhh!" Firestorm shouted, jumping up and down.

Grodd was pleased. "The Justice League fears you. They know what you're capable of and it makes them quiver," he explained. "I, however, would never dream of keeping you from your destiny. There's no need to fear. Embrace your abilities and rule by my side in the new world order."

Suddenly, a group of New York City police officers stormed into the building with their weapons drawn.

"Destroy them!" Grodd commanded. "Use your power."

Firestorm hesitated. He wasn't sure what to do.

"Don't be weak. Do as you're told," Grodd commanded.

Firestorm's eyes turned white. He blasted the police officer's weapons, turning each one into a giant tarantula.

"Get it off me!" an officer shouted.

"Very good," whispered Grodd.

Firestorm aimed his power at a patch of ceiling, changing it into lava. It dripped to the ground, burning holes in the floor. The officers raced from the library for safety.

"You're learning," Grodd said. "Now unleash your full potential."

"Resist Grodd's power, Ronald," said Professor Stein, deep within his brain. "Don't give in."

Firestorm tackled Grodd, pinning him to the ground.

"Me . . . better than . . . you, Grodd," Firestorm growled. "Not . . . your . . . slave!"

"Oh, but you *are*," Grodd said. He used his helmet to blast Firestorm with pure mental energy, throwing him against the wall.

As the hot-headed hero stumbled back to his feet, Grodd noticed Firestorm's hand. It was glowing with power. Sensing trouble, Grodd leaped overhead and onto a swinging chandelier.

"If you use your powers to destroy my helmet, you and your friends will be trapped in your gorilla bodies forever," Grodd said.

Firestorm changed the chandelier into a giant inflatable ball with Grodd trapped inside. It dropped to the ground, bouncing him across the room.

"RARGH!" Grodd screamed, bursting from the ball. "You've tried my patience for the last time." He promptly jolted Firestorm to regain control.

Firestorm's body trembled. His mind raced. Professor Stein's pleas were drowned out by Grodd's overwhelming power.

"You . . . my . . . master . . . forever," Firestorm said.

Oh dear, thought Professor Stein. *This is truly the end. Ronald's mind is lost forever.*

"Bow before me, you stupid, puny human," growled Grodd.

Firestorm shuffled towards his new master until they were face to face.

"Tricked you," Firestorm whispered. He jabbed Grodd in the stomach, causing him to double over in pain.

"Get the helmet!" cried Professor Stein.

"On it, Professor," Firestorm said, snatching Grodd's helmet and placing it on his head. "Now what?"

"Give me a moment. I'm unfamiliar with the inner workings of such a strange device," said Professor Stein. "It's clearly advanced. Quite fascinating, actually."

Grodd was slowly regaining his strength.

"We don't have time, Professor!" cried Firestorm. He focused his mental power into the helmet and a rush of information flooded into his brain.

"I've got it," he whispered. "I know how to defeat him." He faced down Grodd and directed the full force of the helmet's energy towards the weakened gorilla.

"Noooooo!" Grodd roared. His body trembled as his eyes widened in shock. The blast hadn't simply confused him, it had replaced his mind with that of an ordinary gorilla. "Oook?" Grodd said pitifully.

"Not so stupid and puny after all, huh?" said Firestorm. "Now to turn my friends back to normal."

Firestorm concentrated once again as the helmet sent out a pulse of energy. It blanketed the area and returned his teammates to their human forms. The stunned heroes soon joined him at the library.

"Nice work, Firestorm," said Wonder Woman, patting him on the back.

"The kid did it!" Green Arrow said. "Who would have guessed it?"

"I couldn't have done it without the help of Professor Stein," Firestorm said.

Green Lantern used his ring to connect to the Watchtower where Batman was anxiously awaiting his message. "What's happening down there?" he asked.

"We had a few issues, but everything is cool now," Green Lantern said.

"There's a maximum-security cell being prepared for Grodd at Iron Heights Penitentiary," said Batman. "They're waiting for you."

"We'll drop him off and head back to the Watchtower," said Green Lantern.

"Tell me something. Did everyone end up getting along?" Batman asked.

Wonder Woman, Firestorm, Vixen, Green Lantern, Hawkman and Green Arrow erupted with laughter.

"I'll take that as a yes," said Batman.

⟨ END ⟩

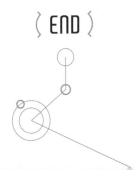

{ TARGET: APPREHENDED }

GORILLA GRODD

Grodd comes from Gorilla City. This secret world in Africa is filled with super intelligent gorillas who live together in peace. That is, when Grodd isn't controlling them with his mind. Not only does Grodd have enhanced strength, he's a master of mind games. He's worked with both the Secret Society and the Legion of Doom, though he prefers to plot alone. Having suffered many defeats at the hands of the Justice League, Grodd harbours an intense hatred for its heroes.

LEX LUTHOR   THE JOKER   CHEETAH   SINESTRO   CAPTAIN COLD

BLACK MANTA

AMAZO

GORILLA GRODD

STAR SAPPHIRE

BRAINIAC

DARKSEID

HARLEY QUINN

BIZARRO

THE SHADE

MONGUL

POISON IVY

MR. FREEZE

COPPERHEAD

ULTRA-
HUMANITE

CAPTAIN
BOOMERANG

SOLOMON GRUNDY

BLACK ADAM

DEADSHOT

CIRCE

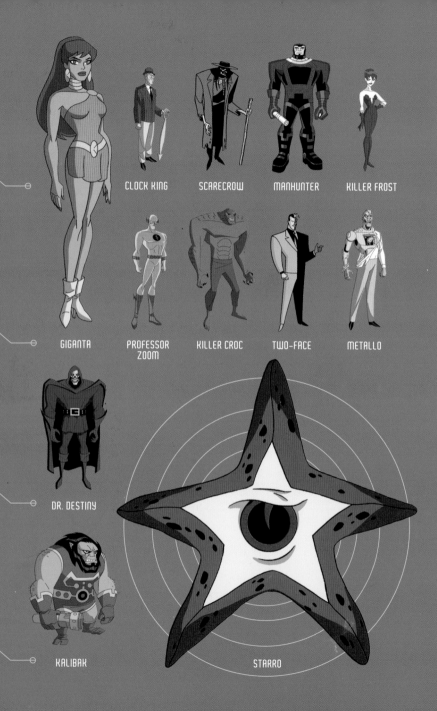

CLOCK KING

SCARECROW

MANHUNTER

KILLER FROST

GIGANTA

PROFESSOR
ZOOM

KILLER CROC

TWO-FACE

METALLO

DR. DESTINY

KALIBAK

STARRO

STRENGTH IN NUMBERS

raintree

a Capstone company—publishers for children

GLOSSARY

channel convey or direct one thing into another

hologram image made by laser beams that looks three-dimensional

insecurity personal characteristic that someone feels anxious or unsure about

instinct behaviour that is natural rather than learned

manipulate influence people to do what you want

molecule group of atoms making up the smallest unit of a substance

stealth ability to move secretly

transform make a great change in something

transmute change the form, appearance or nature of something

telepathic able to communicate from one mind to another without speech or signs

teleport transport by instantly disappearing from one place and reappearing in another